SHAUNA CAGAN

ADDIE AND THE AMAZING ACROBATS

That's me!

Hippo Park

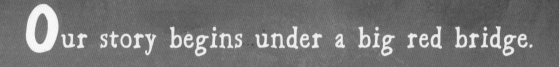

Our story begins under a big red bridge.

Um, excuse me?

Yes, Addie?

BEST BEST FRIENDS!

Ahem. Addie, can we please continue?

Oh, sorry!
Please, do go on!

This is the story of three **BEST** friends.
They were together from the start.

FIRST DAY!

FIRST TOOTH!

(not yet

FIRST BOOK!

FIRST SLEEPOVER!
(stayed up all day)

Their favorite thing was flying.
Addie, Ben, and Jude swooped, flipped,
and somersaulted the nights away.
Especially Addie. Her aerial stunts
were simply spectacular.

Ben became known as
"The Big Flipper."

Jude was "The Comet."

And Addie?
Well, everybody just called her
"The Superstar."

Night after night they
performed their amazing moves.
They soon became . . . .

The "Who Flew By?"

Just WOW!

AMAZING ACROBATS

The "Sky Flop"

The "Inside Outer"

The "Fly-By"

So cool!

Before long, word began to spread
and the crowds grew.

One evening, after a sensational
show, Addie felt a tap on her wing.

Flipper
von Swoopsalot

Come and join the
legendary BIG BAT CIRCUS!
We leave tomorrow
at 6 a.m. sharp!

Addie, Ben, and Jude were over the moon! They were packed and ready to go at 6 a.m. on the dot.

Let the adventures begin!

But things didn't go exactly as planned.

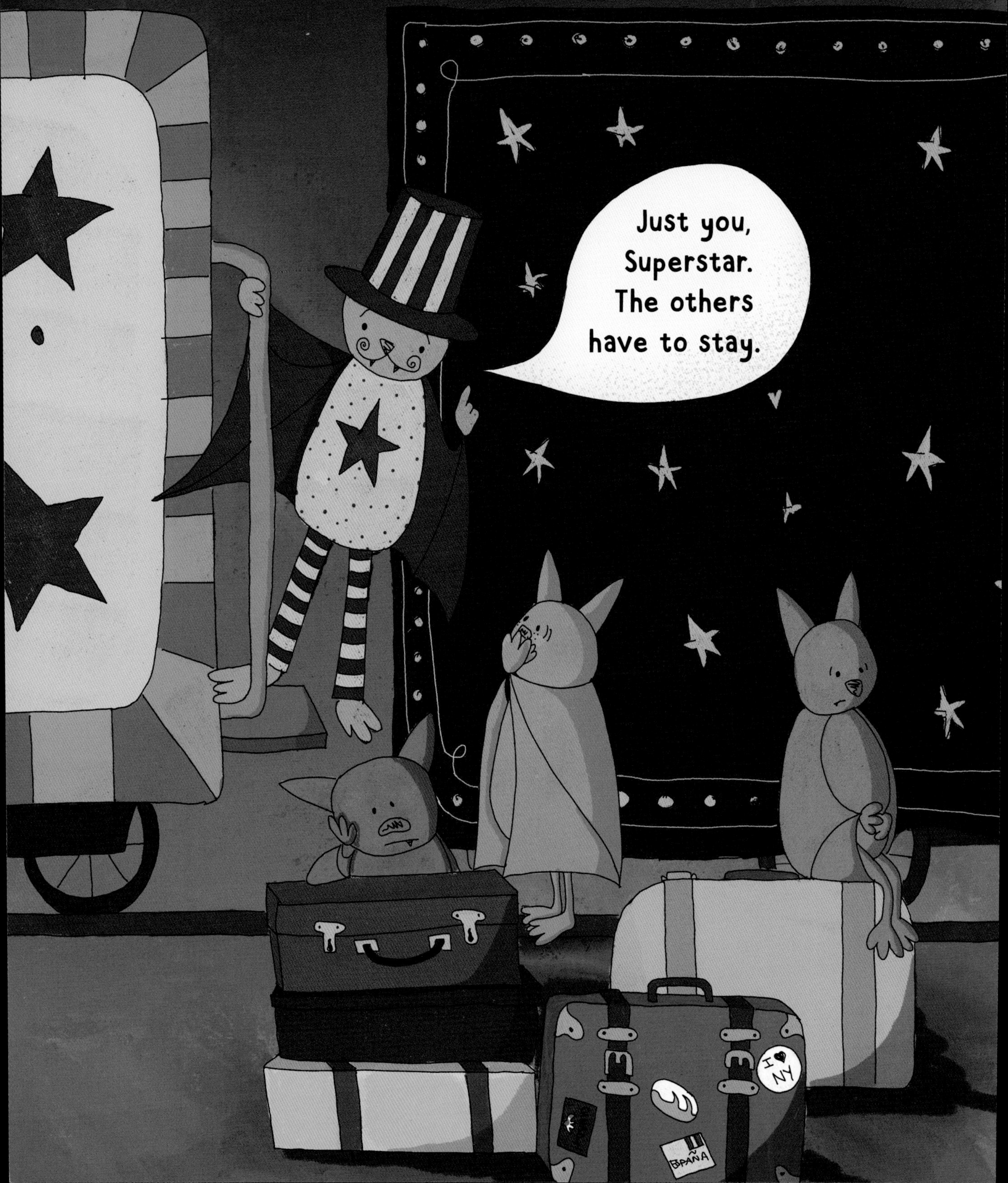

Addie did not know what to do.
This was her chance to be famous! But go
without her buddies? Her best best buddies?

I thought and thought and of course, I decided that I could never leave Ben and Jude to chase fame and glory!

End of story.

Addie, what really happened?

Oh, Addie.

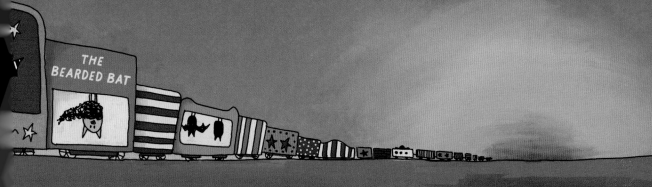

So Addie began her life as a real circus
acrobat. Night after night she
dazzled her fans.

spotlight
(very important)

day vision
goggles!

shiny cape!

sequin boots

But as the weeks went on,
Addie felt like things weren't
quite right.

Something was missing.

Meanwhile, back at the big red bridge, the
Amazing Acrobats did their best to carry on
without Addie, but it wasn't the same.

Her replacement
wasn't working out so
well either.

One day, Addie got some big news.
She wrote to her friends right away.

DEAR BEST FRIENDS,

THE CIRCUS WILL BE
TRAVELING OVER THE
BIG RED BRIDGE IN TWO
TUESDAYS. WE CAN
WAVE HELLO! I WOULD
SO LOVE TO SEE YOU.

YOUR BEST BUDDY,
ADDIE

P.S. I MISS US.

TICKETS
$2.75

But after she mailed her letter, Addie felt a bit uneasy.

Will Ben and Jude come to see me? Are they still even my best best friends?

BIG BAT CIRCUS

When the second Tuesday arrived,
Addie's stomach filled with butterflies.

The train rolled onto the big red bridge
and Addie peeked out.

There was the dark night sky
and a few stars . . .
but no Ben and no Jude.

Addie's heart was broken.
She started working on her next trick.

But then came a TAP TAP TAP.
She looked outside . . .

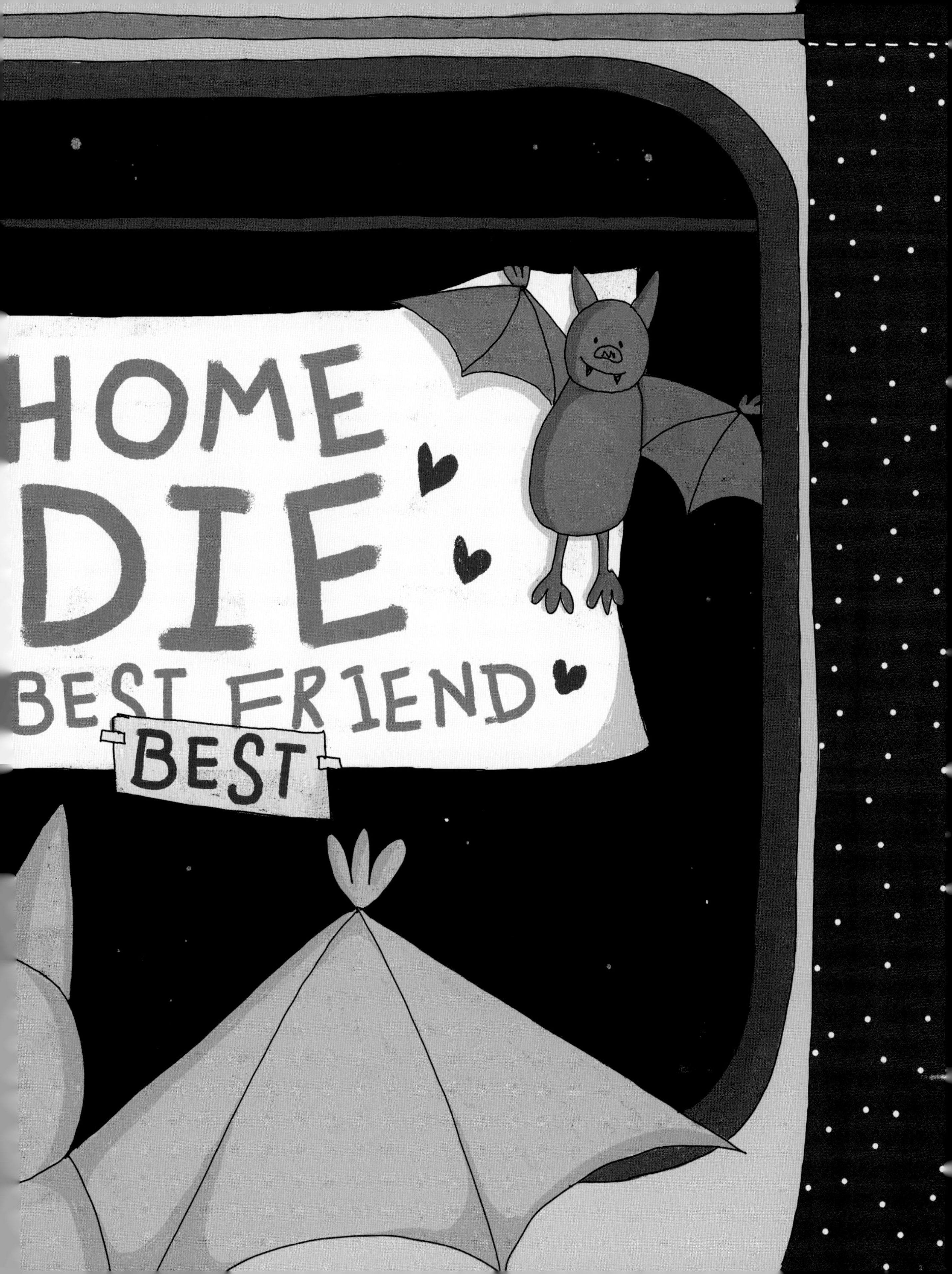
HOME
DIE
BEST FRIEND
BEST

Addie dashed off the train into the
wings of her best friends.
At last she felt like a true star.

Soon the circus was on its way
again. Tearful goodbyes were said.
After all, the show must go on . . .

. . . one way or another.

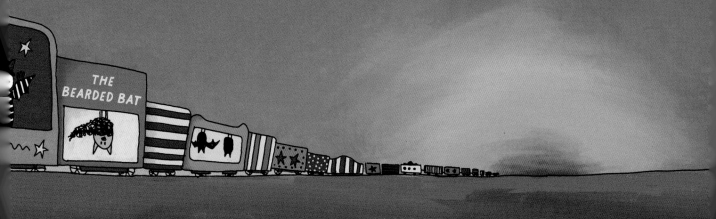

This is the story of three **BEST** friends . . .
back together at last.

FIRST NIGHT
BACK TOGETHER

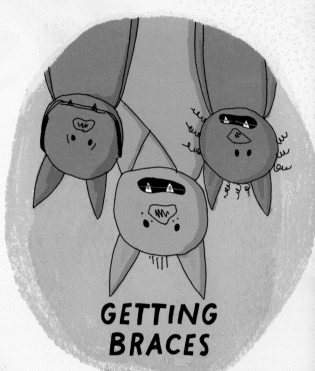

GETTING
BRACES

NEW FAVORITE
BOOK

BEST SLEEPOVER
EVER

And of course, their favorite thing
to do together was still performing.
But now...

...with a grand finale.

The "Best Friends Forever Even When One Joined the Circus and the Other Two Had to Stay Home."

For my family, who made me into me.
For Jill and Amelia, who made this book into this book.
For Mona, who found me. For my writing group, Marilyn,
Theresa, Kathy, Naomi, and Brian, for sticking with me.
And of course for David; you can read me anything.

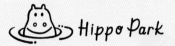 Hippo Park

An imprint of Astra Books for Young Readers,
a division of Astra Publishing House
astrapublishinghouse.com
Printed in China

ISBN: 978-1-6626-4046-9 (hc)
ISBN: 978-1-6626-4047-6 (eBook)
Library of Congress Control Number: 2022947164

First edition
10 9 8 7 6 5 4 3 2 1

Design by Amelia Mack and Shauna Cagan
The text is set in Riley, Fandango, and Custard Cream.
The illustrations are done digitally in Procreate.

The "Lone Wolf"

Awesome Cape

Cool Boots

The "Tic-Tac-Toe"

The "All For One"

The "Three's Company"

The "New Guy"

The "Stop and Go"

Bling Boots